CHRISTMAS

Sue Carabine

Illustrations by
Shauna Mooney Kawasaki

SALT LAKE CITY

For my dear grandchildren:
Adam, Andy, Sarah, Rachael,
Alex, Cate, and Aubrey
– SC –

For all the grandmas in my life
– SMK –

02 01 00   5 4

Copyright © 1998 Gibbs Smith, Publisher

Designed by Mary Ellen Thompson,
TTA Designs
Printed in Hong Kong

Published by
Gibbs Smith, Publisher
P.O. Box 667
Layton, Utah 84041

ISBN 0-87905-820-X
10-copy prepack ISBN 0-87905-244-9

'Twas the night
before Christmas,
the kids had just left,
And Grandma sat down
in her chair for a rest.

She'd hugged them and
kissed them and
waved them good-bye,
Then with a smile on her face
she had breathed a great sigh.

She could still see
the grins on their bright,
shining faces,
See them wiggle and giggle
as she tied their shoelaces.

She thought of
her daughter, their mom,
who had fumed
Because of the candy
her kids had consumed.

How she'd begged
and she'd pleaded,
"Please, Grandma, no more.
If Cate has had one piece of
fudge, she's had four!

Do you suppose
Aubrey will sleep
through this night?
Her tummy's so full
that her jammies are tight."

But Grandma just nodded
and winked at her dears.
After all, Christmastime
comes just once every year.

If she couldn't spoil them
'twould be a great shame.
So she smiled a sweet smile
and accepted the blame.

It was right at this moment
that Santa flew by;
He knew what dear Grandma
was up to and why.

He'd silently watched her
prepare for the season
As she tirelessly shopped and
baked treats for one reason:

Those dear little grandkids
were to her all that mattered,
Though her feet got quite sore
and her apron got spattered.

The gifts that she'd sought
must be perfectly right
So that in each child's eyes
she would see pure delight—

An expression that said,
"Grandma, how did you know
That this was the one gift
that I wanted so?"

Ah! Grandmas just know this,
Santa thought to himself,
Why—doesn't my dear
Mrs. Claus know each elf?

And doesn't she also know
children worldwide
And how they are feeling
way deep down inside?

That is why grandmas
know just what is right
To give to their dear ones
this glorious night.

So thinking, old Santa
flew up on his way,
He had so much to tend to
before Christmas Day.

He left Grandma sitting
there sorting the gifts,
Selecting the gift wrap
small spirits to lift.

Adam, the teenager,
knew his gift was clothes,
So he couldn't care less
which gift wrap she chose.

She knew that sweet Sarah
and Rachael would squeal
Ripping open their gifts,
seeing what they revealed.

Then Andy, dear Andy,
so easy to please,
Would run and kiss Grandma
and jump on her knees,

Saying, "Oh, how I wish
that each single day
was awesome as Christmas.
I want it to stay!"

This kind little thought
that young Andy'd express
Was what Santa was thinking
as he put on his vest,

"Why can't folks be generous
and loving all year,
Not only at Christmas?"
he said to his deer.

"What a wonderful place
this old world would be!"
Mrs. Claus, who stood close,
whispered, "Yes, I agree!

"Why don't you inquire
of some grandmas tonight
Just how they spread happiness,
cheer, and delight.

"What makes them persist
and expect no return
And love so completely
even if they are spurned?"

"What an excellent notion,"
St. Nick cried with glee.
"Without you, my sweet wife,
where on earth would I be?"

And so Santa set off,
a new spring in his step—
Even Dasher and Dancer
and the crew had more pep!

The gifts for the first stop
he gently set down,
Then, carefully, with keen eyes
he scanned the whole town.

He soon saw a
grandmother sitting alone,
Focusing on a small voice
on the phone.

With a wink of his eye
and a nod of his head,
He joined that sweet grandma
and heard what she said:

"Oh, Alex, I wish
I could be with you too,
But I know what you'd like
and I've mailed it to you.

"Look out at the snowflakes—
as light as a feather—
Each one means I love you
and we'll soon be together."

Santa knew without asking
one answer he sought:
That some gifts from grandmas
could never be bought.

He flew up and away
the next village to visit,
Over sparkling, snow-
covered trees so exquisite.

He delivered his load
and spied a great house
Where a well-to-do grandma
sat quiet as a mouse.

He stopped by to ask
with what problem she toiled,
Was surprised when she said,
"My grandchildren are spoiled.

So this year we're giving
and sharing our toys,
Having fun bringing joy
to some sick girls and boys."

Nick then found a grandma
in a home, oh so small,
Who was rollicking
with grandkids—
they were having a ball!

They romped on her couch
full of patches and splits,
But when you're with Grandma
it feels like the Ritz.

The last sweet old lady
he met on the way home,
Was one among many
who also played Mom.

She cared for these youngsters
from eight until five,
Never complaining,
just helping them thrive.

Finally dear Santa
zoomed back to the Pole.
He had an idea
to reward the dear souls.

By magic he contacted
children worldwide,
"Send love notes to Grandma
and thank her," he cried.

The children were happy
to please old St. Nick,
For he was their hero
(he'd brought them great gifts).

So the following day,
when grandmas awoke,
Tears ran down their cheeks
as they read a sweet note.

All of the children of all
different ages
Wrote "I LOVE YOU"
to Grandma
on pages and pages.

And as for the grandmas,
this Christmas
would give
Some beautiful memories
as long as they lived

Of love notes and wishes
from Nick, who took flight:
"Merry Christmas,
dear grandmas.
Sleep soundly tonight."